Dear Parents:

Congratulations! Your child is taking the first steps on an exciting journey. The destination? Independent reading!

STEP INTO READING® will help your child get there. The program offers five steps to reading success. Each step includes fun stories and colorful art or photographs. In addition to original fiction and books with favorite characters, there are Step into Reading Non-Fiction Readers, Phonics Readers and Boxed Sets, Sticker Readers, and Comic Readers—a complete literacy program with something to interest every child.

Learning to Read, Step by Step!

Ready to Read   Preschool–Kindergarten
• big type and easy words • rhyme and rhythm • picture clues
For children who know the alphabet and are eager to begin reading.

Reading with Help   Preschool–Grade 1
• basic vocabulary • short sentences • simple stories
For children who recognize familiar words and sound out new words with help.

Reading on Your Own   Grades 1–3
• engaging characters • easy-to-follow plots • popular topics
For children who are ready to read on their own.

Reading Paragraphs   Grades 2–3
• challenging vocabulary • short paragraphs • exciting stories
For newly independent readers who read simple sentences with confidence.

Ready for Chapters   Grades 2–4
• chapters • longer paragraphs • full-color art
For children who want to take the plunge into chapter books but still like colorful pictures.

STEP INTO READING® is designed to give every child a successful reading experience. The grade levels are only guides; children will progress through the steps at their own speed, developing confidence in their reading. The F&P Text Level on the back cover serves as another tool to help you choose the right book for your child.

Remember, a lifetime love of reading starts with a single step!

PHOEBE DUNN was a world-renowned photographer known especially for her pictures of children and animals. Her timeless images, photographed in natural settings, using natural light, uniquely capture the interactions and relationships between children and their pets. Phoebe photographed the world as she knew it, capturing the feelings and relationships that make us all human. Her photographs have been published around the world in more than twenty children's books, a number of them written by her daughter, Judy Dunn.

Text copyright © 1980, 2016 by Judy Dunn Spangenberg
Cover and interior photographs copyright © 2016 by The Phoebe Dunn Collection, LLC

Visit us on the Web!
StepIntoReading.com
randomhousekids.com

Educators and librarians, for a variety of teaching tools, visit us at
RHTeachersLibrarians.com

Library of Congress Cataloging-in-Publication Data
Dunn, Judy.
The little rabbit / by Judy Dunn ; photographs by Phoebe Dunn. — Abridged edition.
pages cm. — (Step into reading. Step 1)
"This is an abridged edition of The Little Rabbit, originally published by Random House Children's Books, New York, in 1980."
Summary: Sarah's Easter gift rabbit becomes her constant companion and eventually gives birth to seven little bunnies.
ISBN 978-0-553-53354-5 (trade pbk.) — ISBN 978-0-553-53355-2 (lib. bdg.)
[1. Rabbits as pets—Fiction.] I. Dunn, Phoebe. II. Title.
PZ7.D92158Li 2016 [E]—dc23 2014040441

Printed in the United States of America 10 9 8 7 6 5 4 3 2 1

This book has been officially leveled by using the F&P Text Level Gradient™ System.

The Little Rabbit

by Judy Dunn

photographs by Phoebe Dunn

Random House 🏠 New York

Sarah found
a little rabbit
in her Easter basket.

The rabbit was soft
and white.

Sarah named her
Buttercup.

She took good care of Buttercup.

Sarah's friends loved
Buttercup.

Buttercup was happy

to be around people.

Sarah took her
to the meadow.

Buttercup made new
friends.

A turtle.

A butterfly.

Buttercup saw something moving.

It was another rabbit.

It began to rain.

Buttercup ran for cover.

She was lost!

Sarah found Buttercup.
She put her
in her backpack.

She fed her a carrot.

Buttercup began to grow and grow.

She was going

to have babies.

She made a nest
for them.

One morning
Sarah looked
into the hutch.

The baby rabbits
had been born!

Buttercup was
a good mom.

The bunnies liked
to sit in Sarah's lap.

The bunnies
were growing
too big for the hutch.

Good homes
were found for them.

Sarah's friends
Billy and Kate
each took one.

Jeff took two.

Sarah and Buttercup
were happy.

"I love you, Buttercup!"